www.fast-print.net/store.php

Red Flame: Wizards' School
Copyright © Pamela Shine 2012

ISBN 978-178035-422-4

First published 2012 by
FASTPRINT PUBLISHING
Peterborough, England.

Author's Biography

I am 12 years old and I was born in Hackney, east London. I lived in Hackney until I was seven years old and for the last five years I have been living with my family in Shoeburyness, Southend-on-Sea, Essex.

This is the first book I have written and I plan to write sequels. I hope, therefore, that you will enjoy reading my book.

Chapter 1:

The Fateful Encounter

"Hi, my name is Resha, Resha Valentine. I
live in the Canory County. Right now I'm in
Blue-Bell City. It's a great place, but I
dream of entering a school. To people
where you live school is a drag, but I live on
Wizland. Wizland is a place where humans
and the mythological world live in
harmony... meaning wizards! Most schools
on Wizland are for wizards to learn about
their magic and be sent on a job to use their
magic. If they complete their job they get
money rewards! The jobs are requested by
people without magic energy and are sent to
the school asking for wizards to fulfil these

jobs. The school I want to join is a top notch school! Many legends in Wizland started out in this school. The school is called Red Flame! But standards have dropped. Just last week a girl with red hair and a boy with black hair with red flame marks were seen destroying a whole village! But I still want to join so badly!"

One day I was walking through the streets looking for magic shops. But instead I found a crowd surrounding a guy. The guy was supposed to be the flame ruler. The flame ruler is a powerful wizard who uses magic you can't buy in stores. This man was weird but for some reason my heart fluttered. "What is this feeling?" I said. "Could it be...? Am I in love?"

Suddenly someone shouted out "KAT!" At that moment I returned to my normal self. I realised instantly that it was a charm spell. Once the person who is being controlled by a charm spell knows about the spell they can no longer be affected by it.

I spun around on my heels to see who had broken the spell on me. Pushing his way through the crowds was a boy with black hair and green eyes. He was wearing a black t-shirt with a big yellow star on it. He looked eager to get to the front of the crowd. When he reached the front, which had taken a surprisingly shorter time than when I was pushing through the crowds, he looked at the flame ruler.

His expression changed from eager to confused. "Who are you?" he asked. The flame ruler looked shocked and the crowd attacked the boy. As the entire crowd were girls the dude couldn't hit back.

"Now, now, ladies leave the poor boy alone," the flame ruler said. As soon as that came out of his mouth the girls were drooling all over him. Then the flame ruler clicked his fingers and fire sent him flying into the sky. When he left the spell was broken and the crowd left. The boy who had ran through the crowd was laying on the floor shocked at what had just happened and for some reason I felt like he was angry too. I walked up to him and introduced myself and explained that he had broken a spell that was cast on me. I then invited him to eat lunch with me as a thank you.

When we reached the restaurant he ate a lot! It looked like he hadn't eaten in weeks! "It's because I haven't," he said.

"I didn't say anything," I responded surprised.

"Err... no, I'm pretty sure you did," he added less confidently.

"So what sort of cat are you looking for?"

"Kat is not a cat. She's my sister," he said ignorantly. "Oh, and you thought that she was in that crowd?"

"No, she wouldn't be drooling over a fake-o like that. She would be beating the life outta him," he said with a smirk. I sat back in my chair as he continued eating. *This guy may have saved me from that spell but he is weird.*

"My name is... Aiden Flamebuster by the... way," he managed to say while eating.

"Well I had better be leaving." I put down the money to pay for the meal on the table. As I was leaving, people from other tables were making faces. I turned round to find the boy bowing.

"THANK YOU FOR THE MEAL," he shouted.

I screamed and responded "It's ok you helped me and now we are even."

I ran out of the restaurant. When I got outside I breathed a huge sigh of relief as I knew I wouldn't be seeing him again. I started walking away. I didn't know it at the time but as I was walking I had passed Aiden's twin, Kat.

Later on that day I was sitting on a park bench thinking of what Red Flame must be like. What sort of people go there, what magic is theirs? I was thrilled at the thought of joining. I wrote down my feelings in a notepad that I carried with me everywhere I went. I brushed my blonde hair behind my ear as I was writing. I don't know why but it seemed to be a habit. I tugged at my blue skirt as I was thinking of what to write. This was another one of my habits. Suddenly a smell entered the atmosphere. IT WAS A SLEEP SPELL! But it was too late. I had already inhaled it and had fallen fast asleep.

When I woke up I was tied to a chair. I couldn't move at all. What had happened? Don't tell me someone had found out after only two months? I looked up and saw no-one other than the flame ruler! I was confused. If he was a good guy why would he tie me up? I hoped he hadn't found out my secret. I tried to untie my hands.

"It's useless," he said. "But knock yourself out... Resha Valentine!" Oh no! He had found out! But I didn't get it! I'd made sure no-one found out my second name! Not even Aiden! I calmed down and looked around. The room was swaying and there were sounds coming from the door.

"Turn to starboard. All hands on deck!" It was easy to tell that I was on a boat. Wait a Boat? Oh no, they were told to find me! There was a big crash. Everything outside went quiet and the boat swayed even more than before.

Then there was another crash. The ceiling broke and a girl with red hair, a fringe covering her left eye and what looked like goggles keeping her hair up came crashing in followed by a boy with black hair. I couldn't make out their faces in the darkness. The boy ran over and untied me. As he was closer I could see his face. It was Aiden! The Flame Ruler then threw fire at us. We were going to be burnt to a cinder! Of all of a sudden we went shooting into the air!

I looked at Aiden. Behind him was what looked like wings made of stars! I was thinking of what to ask him. "I'll explain once we make it to shore," he said. He was looking at the boat. It looked like he was concerned. When we made it to shore I was about to ask him some questions but suddenly the boat that I was on came crashing ashore. Luckily Aiden had pulled me out of the way and we were flying again.

The boat was covered with flames and half of the city had been destroyed. Out of the flames you could see the girl with red hair standing on the ship.

"You say you're from Red Flame...well it's no use to you as you're about to die," the flame ruler boasted. He shot fire at the girl.

I screamed "RUN!" But Aiden hushed me.

"Just watch," he said. The fire ruler turned to leave.

A strange swishing noise came from the flames. "Are you sure you're a fire wizard? Because these are some nasty flames!" In the fire you could just make out the girl's outline. Suddenly most of the flames vanished and you could see the girl EATING

THE FIRE!!! She ate all of it. "Now I've had something to eat, I'm all fired up!" she smirked.

"See, that girl! Red hair, demon eyes, eats fire, she's the real deal! She's... the Flame Ruler," I said astonished. The fake flame ruler tried to escape but the girl boosted herself towards him using flames.

"FIRE MAGIC: FLAMING FIST!" she shouted. Her fist set alight and she hit the dude in the face which knocked him into a building! Aiden lowered me down to the ground.

I looked around and realised that they were the girl and boy from Red Flame. I looked at Aiden and saw on his right shoulder the Red Flame mark and the girl had hers on her right cheek. I looked back at the city and said "You over did it."

The whole city was destroyed! There were flames everywhere! I heard what sounded like an army coming. Suddenly something ran past me so fast I didn't see what it was. It grabbed my arms and pulled me.

"Hey! What are you doing?!" I screamed.

"You want to join Red Flame right?" The girl's head turned around. I was surprised that she knew that. "My name's Kat," she smiled. "Come join Red Flame!"

My face turned to a smile automatically. "Okay! Let's go!" And we kept running to Red Flame Wizard School!

Chapter 2:
The Flame Twins

We gave up on running when we had
outrun the army. I knew it would be a long
walk to Red Flame but it was a good thing
as I had a lot to ask them. Like what was
Red Flame like? How did they get in? What
did I have to do to get in? What magic did
they use? What sort of people were in Red
Flame? Would I fit in? Do they always
wreck villages? Was it a habit of theirs? I
was sure they would have a lot of questions
for me too. But whenever I tried asking
they simply responded "Maybe later. Not
now. That's Private. You'll be fine." I never

got a word in. They never answered any of my questions and they never asked me any.

But they were funny. We ran out of food by the time we got to a river and Aiden decided to catch some fish. The first few goes he got nothing, but Kat kept saying "Don't give up, you'll get one soon." And when there was no hope of any fish he caught a huge fish but then, when he was holding it, it bit his head and his head was completely in its mouth. He started running around with no sense of where he was going. Kat was no help as she was rolling on the floor laughing. And I was chasing after him telling him to stop. He ran into a tree and the fish let go. Kat couldn't stop laughing for the rest of the night. But to be fair I was also secretly laughing.

We kept walking. The woods seemed to get scarier and scarier. Kat picked up on the fact that I was scared and played a trick on me. She snuck away and when she was out of sight she screamed and made a weird dragon-like noise. Aiden didn't know it was a joke, just like me. He grabbed my arm and ran towards where Kat's scream came from. Kat had made a scary mask made of grass and leaves by the time we reached where the scream came from, we started to look around. Aiden was obviously worried, after all Kat was his twin sister even if they didn't look alike. I stayed near Aiden all the time. I may be a wizard but I didn't think my magic was very powerful. Suddenly Kat jumped out with the mask on and made the dragon-like noise again. I tripped over a rock and accidentally pushed over Aiden. The end result was me on top of Aiden on the floor.

Aiden was blushing when he realised what happened, and so was I. Kat burst into laughter and started to roll on the floor. Aiden and I got up and looked at Kat. At first I wanted to kill her. But I started to laugh. Aiden looked at me and Kat, and he also started laughing. I'm probably exaggerating but I swear we were laughing for the whole day. The twins sure are strange yet they complement each other so well. In a way I'm kind of jealous. Jealous... that they have such a great bond as a family. Whereas I...   '

After a long journey we arrived in Jorona, the city where Red Flame was stationed. The city looked wonderful from the outside. When we got there the streets were filled with life that is until the people saw Kat and Aiden. They all went silent and made a path down the middle of the street. Kat and Aiden looked at the people on both sides of the street and laughed. "They heard about it already?" laughed Aiden.

"Talk about nosy," sniggered Kat. They started walking down the path.

I had stopped to look around at the time so I had to run to catch up. When I was nearly by them again someone grabbed me.

"Ha ha look what I got," sniggered the teenage boy who had grabbed me.

"Let's have some fun," said another. Suddenly Kat punched one of them in the face. Even without magic that hit sent the boy flying!

"Hurry up slow poke," she smirked while walking away. Again, I ran after both her and Aiden.

We continued walking for a while. But after a few minutes of walking I heard people whispering.

"The flame twins are back."

"They brought a girl with them."

"Poor dear. She doesn't know what she's doing."

"I pity her!" What did these comments mean? I knew that these two were bad news but surely not that bad!

I ignored the snide comments and kept walking so I wouldn't be caught in another awkward situation. Soon we were at the end of the path. There were a few steps going up and a huge gate. At the top of the gate was a banner with the Red Flame mark on it. I smiled. I was finally here. At Red Flame Wizards' School.

Chapter 3:

Meeting and Greeting

I followed Kat and Aiden into Red Flame. I was surprised no-one was in the grounds. It was completely empty. Kat and Aiden stopped.

"Do you think?" Aiden gulped. "They have found out?"

"Think Positive," Kat said, giving a false smile. I was starting to get worried. Found out what? About Blue-Bell City? What was going to happen?

We continued to walk. We entered the building. Everything was quiet. I was a tad worried. Aiden's expression looked concerned. We were walking up to what was called 'The Main Room'. Everyone in a wizards' school spends most their time here, except when in lessons of course.

The Main Room is where you accept jobs, chat with friends and pretty much everything else other than learning. When you no longer need to learn how to control your magic you graduate. When you graduate in Wizland you don't have to leave school. You can stay in school but you don't have to attend lessons. Meaning you spend 100% of your time in the Main Room or doing jobs.

Kat and Aiden looked at each other. They both rested their hands on the handles. There was a pause and they opened the door. Behind the door were loads of Red Flame members. They were all looking at Kat and Aiden. They all looked angry and then they all smiled and said "welcome back!" Suddenly a banner flopped down from the ceiling. It read 'Congrats on your 100th job.'

"Yeah, they've found out," groaned Kat. "All hell is going to break loose now." Suddenly there was confetti everywhere and people were laughing and dancing.

"God save us," groaned Aiden. Suddenly Aiden and Kat were grabbed and were made to start dancing.

I started to laugh really, really hard. Before I knew the music had been cut and everyone was staring at me. I didn't know what to do. I felt so out of place. Kat and Aiden stood next to me and said "Welcome Resha, the new member of Red Flame!" Suddenly there was a silence.

Kat stepped forward and asked "You got a problem with that?" Everyone, but Aiden, was scared including me.

"No, we don't have a problem with that," replied one girl.

"Welcome Resha!" said another person. The celebration continued.

Someone changed the banner to 'Congrats on your 100th job and welcome to Red Flame Resha!' After a while of celebrating a boy entered. He had dark blue hair. Considering what I had just seen I would have thought he was normal, if he had had a top on! His Red Flame mark was on his chest. Kat had hers on her right cheek. I was wondering where to have mine put.

The boy walked over to Aiden and said, "Hey idiot I'll smash you to pieces."

"Bring it Lucas! That is if you have it!" replied Aiden. Kat bashed their heads together.

"Grow up will you!" Aiden and Lucas then fell to the floor.

"But you fight with Lilith all the time!" shouted Aiden and Lucas.

"Well she asks for it!" Kat shouted back.

"Is there a sane person in this place?" I said to myself.

"Hi there!" I turned to see a girl in complete orange with a boy in green. "My name's Layla and this is Ethan." She smiled cheerfully, "We're from team rainbow!"

"Team Rainbow?" I asked confused.

"In schools you make groups with people and go on jobs with them. Our group includes three people. Us two and Lilith."

"Really?" I questioned with great interest.

I got out my notepad and wrote down what Layla said about the teams. "Yeah by the looks of things you're with team Fire Star."

I looked up. "Team Fire Star?"

"Yeah, Kat and Aiden's team. Normally they don't get along well with people but they seem to like you," she said. I looked at Kat and Aiden.

"Why are they called team Fire Star?" I asked.

"'Cause of their magic silly! Kat's a fire wizard and Aiden's a star wizard."

"Star wizard? But that's a lost magic!" I replied somewhat surprised.

"Yeah cool right?" responded Layla. "That's why they're the strongest team in Red Flame. If you get in, people think you're super strong."

"I came to Red Flame to learn and earn money; not to be thought of as a strong wizard when all I did was join a strong team," I said.

Suddenly Aiden and Kat started talking.

"Good answer Resha," nodded Aiden.

"Welcome to the team," smiled Kat.

I turned around "HOW LONG HAVE YOU BEEN THERE?" I shouted. Kat and Aiden looked at each other and smiled at me.

"All of it," they grinned.

"Damn it, haven't you ever heard of privacy?" I said angrily.

"Get used to it," they said together. "After all, we're a team now!" they laughed.

"What did I do wrong to deserve this?" I whispered to myself. "What did I do to get the team which destroys whole villages?"

Chapter 4:
Malica's Dilemma

"It had been a week since I joined Red Flame Wizards' School. It had been a really fun experience! I was doing well in my academic classes and I was about to start my first magic class. I was so excited to show off my magic. My magic is a lost magic like Aiden's. Lost magic is a magic lost to the ages meaning nobody has had that magic for a long, long time."

"Morning everyone!" I said, entering the classroom. Suddenly a bucket of ice cold water dropped on my head.

"Damn it, Resha that was meant for Aiden!" shouted Lucas.

Lucas is a classmate of mine. I met him at the 'Welcome Resha Party'. The first time we talked wasn't so pleasant. At the party he had pulled a prank on me accidentally and he shouted at me for getting in the way. The prank was so harsh that I was reduced to tears. His attitude changed instantly. He asked me to stop crying as if he was too weak to do anything. Then he apologised.

So I pretty much worked out that his weakness is female tears. He also has a habit of taking his top off, no matter what the circumstances are and his favourite pastime is pranking and fighting Aiden. When he found out I was in team Fire Star that didn't really help our relationship either.

"Here you go Resha," said Layla passing me a cloth.

"Thanks Layla," I responded, drying myself off.

"You must be excited, after all this is your first magic lesson!"

"Yeah, I haven't seen everyone's magic yet so it should be fun."

"Okay class take your seats," said Miss Elimenmo (Eli-men-mo). "As we have a new student why don't we show what we have learnt, let's start with Lucas." Lucas stood up and walked to the front. He put his hands together and blew into them. He gave me a rose made of ice. It looked really beautiful.

"Ok, how about you now, Layla?" Lucas sat back down and Layla got up. She waved her pen in the air and the word flowers appeared. It was made of complete flowers and was real! From this you could tell Layla was a writing wizard.

"Okay now you Aiden." Layla sat down and Aiden got up. Like the others he went to the front.

"Star Magic; Starry Eyes," he said. Suddenly loads of stars appeared. They were all so beautiful. He sat down and they disappeared. This chain continued on and on until only one person was left.

"Kat," said Miss Elimenmo. Kat stood up from the back of the classroom. She slowly walked to the front. *Can fire magic really look pretty like the others?* I thought. Everyone was whispering.

"This is going to be really good," said one girl. I couldn't tell if she was being sarcastic or not. Kat stood at the front of the classroom.

She smiled and moved her arms in a circular direction. Suddenly she was surrounded by flames. It didn't look pretty but I wondered what she would do. The fire turned into small flames and Kat was making quick movements. The small flames changed into the shape of flowers and hearts. It was truly the most beautiful one. The flames then disappeared and Kat bowed. The whole class started clapping including me.

"Expected from my best student," responded the teacher. Kat sat down in her seat again.

"Now Resha, would you mind showing us your magic?" asked the teacher. I stood up and heard a voice from a girl at the back.

"If she has any magic that is, she does everything by herself and she's such a klutz," she whispered. A memory ran through my head of someone who was dear to me saying something just like that. I went to the front still thinking of that memory. I turned to face the class and there was a gasp.

I realised that the memory had made me cry. I heard a chair screech and looked to the back. Kat was holding the girl who had talked about me in the air by her collar. "Keep your mouth shut if you don't want to lose it," Kat shouted.

"Ka-" started Miss Elimenmo.

"KAT PUT HER DOWN!" I interrupted. Kat looked at me shocked.

"Don't worry, I'm fine now," I responded with a cheesy smile. Kat dropped the girl and sat back down in her seat.

I breathed a deep breath. I always had roses slotted into a makeshift slot in my belt. I pulled one of the roses out of the slot. "ROSE MAGIC: FLOWER SHIMMER," I said out loud and threw the rose to the ground. As soon as it touched the ground, flower petals and glitter were flying around the class room. The whole class started to clap. I picked up the rose and the petals and the glitter disappeared.

"I'm impressed Resha," said Miss Elimenmo.

I laughed, "Thanks, my magic may not be powerful but it's pretty."

Later on in the Main Room, "I feel like something's been missing over the last week... hmmm help me out Aiden," asked Kat.

"I've had that feeling lately too... I wonder what it is..." replied Aiden.

Lucas walked over and said "Hey, do you guys get the feeling something's missing?"

"Yep," responded Kat and Aiden.

Suddenly a girl with light blue hair and yellow and blue clothes ran in. I had never seen her before but next to her belly button was the Red Flame mark. She was covered in cuts and bruises. "Kat, Aiden, Lucas I need your help!" she panted.

"Malica!" said the three of them.

"That's what was missing," said Kat.

"Urm guys... you're missing the fact she's covered in cuts and bruises." I said. Then there was a short silence.

"Malica what happened to you?" asked Lucas.

"What do you need our help with?" questioned Aiden. *"They're ignoring me, aren't they?"* I said to myself.

"Blue Hawk. They attacked me while I was on a job. They're going to attack the school!" she said.

"Not if we can help it," responded Kat and Aiden.

"This is the first and last time I'm working with this idiot," replied Lucas.

"I've got to help too... right?" I groaned.

"We're a team Resha, so you got to help!" replied the twins.

Chapter 5:

Attack on Red Flame School

Suddenly there was a big crash. It was the front gate! That noise meant all hell was about to break lose. We ran to the front gate as fast as we could. Most of the school had gathered there. Standing at the gate were five people, four boys and one girl. It was going to be a fair five on five battle. That is until they showed Layla tied up and battered. Her siblings and teammates, Ethan and Lilith, ran to her and dragged her to the nurse's room. I looked at Kat. Normally she looked mad and angry but now she was on a whole other level. All of a sudden she was surrounded by flames.

Aiden, Lucas and Malica looked angry too. Lucas attacked the one who seemed like the leader but got hit instead.

"Ha you flames are wimps," said the leader. "I'm Nero from Blue Hawk."

A boy with red hair stepped forward and called himself 'Moonlight'. Then a boy who was really big stepped forward and called himself 'Rocky'. The girl stepped forward and called herself 'Lisa'. Finally the last boy also stepped forward and called himself 'Racer'.

"Okay guys, let's show 'em they can't mess with our school and get away with it! Kat you take Nero, Aiden you get Moonlight, I'll take Rocky, and Lucas you get Lisa, that means you, Resha, have Racer," said Malica.

"As long as I get to kick these punks' butts I'm fine with it!" said Kat racing off. Aiden, Lucas and Malica ran after her.

"But guys I can't fight!" I shouted.

"Then you're pretty much doomed," said Racer. I turned on my heels and kicked him in the face. He fell to the floor.

I grabbed one of my roses. "ROSE MAGIC: EXPLOSION!" and threw the rose at him. He stupidly grabbed the rose and got blown up ten times worse than it would have if it had just hit him. He was knocked out really badly. When that happened I knew these were small fries if I could beat them. I then watched the other fights unravel.

Malica was taking on Rocky, she pulled out some cards. "Card Magic; K.O.," she shouted and threw a card with 'K.O.' written on it at Rocky.   He was slow to dodge it and was knocked out by the card.

Next, I watched Lucas fight. Lisa used water magic and threw boiling water at him sending him flying into the air. It had taken a lot of his magic but he turned the boiling water to ice and Lisa along with it. He broke the ice and she had been knocked out like the others.

Then it was Aiden's fight. His opponent was harder than the others. Aiden had been hit several times. "By the eighty-eight stars of heaven, Galaticas!" Aiden shouted. There was a big light and a huge explosion. Moonlight, like the rest, had been knocked out.

Chapter 6:
Red Rebellion

Nero on the other hand was the toughest by far. Kat had been knocked to the ground.

"Ha you're the legendary Flame Ruler? What a Bluff!" he laughed. Kat stood up and went for another attack but was counter-attacked. She was sent flying but during this time her fringe that covered her left eye never moved. Her goggles came flying off and she was covered in cuts and bruises. By this time everyone had finished their fights and were watching.

"KAT!" shouted Aiden. With all her strength Kat stood up.

"Coward!" she shouted with her head facing the floor. "You wait until I throw my hit until you strike. By that logic you're no better that a goldfish," she laughed. This got Nero angry he ran over to her and punched her in the stomach. She hit the school wall and fell to the ground. But again she stood up. "If that's all the power you've got then this fight's already finished," she said with her head facing the ground.

Kat suddenly looked up. Her fringe was to the side revealing her left eye. It had a scar going over it and then stood up straight with her eyes staring at Nero. She moved her hand in circular motions, like she always did when using magic. "FIRE MAGIC: QUEEN OF FLAME!" she shouted. Her left eye turned dark red, then a tiara made of fire appeared on her head. "Queen Flame Magic: Hell Riser," she said as she

made a cross motion with her arms.
Suddenly the ground underneath Nero
started to crack and flames rose up. Nero
couldn't run, he couldn't hide and he
couldn't counter-attack. The flames were
battering him and then the flames
disappeared and the crack along with it.

Nero was instantly knocked out.
Everyone's attention turned to Kat. "The
queen of flames... a lost magic... she's never
used it... and she never mentioned anything
about that scar," replied Aiden shocked.
The tiara on Kat's head disappeared and her
left eye turned blue again. She collapsed to
the floor with no energy left. Aiden, Lucas,
Malica and I ran over to her and carried her
to the nurse's room.

Chapter 7:

Breathe Normally

When we got to the nurses room the nurse gasped at the sight of the scar. Even though Kat had been in a lot of fights while helping out on jobs was sent to the nurse's office a lot, not even the nurse had seen the scar. When Kat woke up we asked her about the scar but she refused to tell us. "It's a memory best left behind," she would say.

Everyone visited her, even Lucas who grew very respectful of Kat due to the magic power that came off her during the fight. Aiden on the other hand visited less than anyone else. After all, his own twin had been keeping a secret from him.

"Don't worry about them, it's to be expected. Aiden was always an open book to his sister and for him to realise she was keeping something from him would of course make him sad," sighed Malica.

"It just doesn't feel right though!" I moaned. "Even when I had just met them I felt a strong connection between them!" Unexpectedly a girl wearing a black cloak and a piece of cloth that covered her mouth came up behind us.

"This break up spells danger!" she yelled. We looked behind us. "If those two do not unite as one again... Red Flame will be blown out!" she said. "BEWARE!" she backed out of the door.

"Who was that nut job?" I enquired.

"That's Feral. She's a year higher than us," Malica replied looking scared. "Her magic is a lost magic called Time Machine."

I gasped. "That magic can tell the future or see into the past!" I started to shake. "That means she looked into the future and... OH NO!" I shouted.

I ran to the nurse's office and burst in through the door. The bed where Kat was put was empty. I left and started running around the school. I started looking everywhere for Kat and Aiden. By accident I ran into Lucas and we both fell on the floor.

"Hey! What's the big idea?" he yelled. "Watch where ya..." he stared at me. "What's wrong? You look scared," he asked whilst looking concerned.

"Girl... Time Machine... Red Flame... Aiden... Kat...Finished..." I said trying to catch my breath.

"Whoa slow down," he responded, helping me up.

"Feral used Time Machine Magic to see into the future. She said if Aiden and Kat don't make up... Red Flame is finished..."

Lucas was shocked. "Damn Aiden, why can't you just make up with your sister?" Lucas shouted. "Ok, you go look on the roof top and I'll look in the grounds," he said. We started to run in different directions.

"Kat! Aiden! Where are you? I've only just joined Red Flame and now it's going to disappear. I've done everything to get here. Being here is my dream. I've met so many good people on the way. I even made friends here. Real friends..." I said to myself. "AND I'M NOT GONNA LOSE THEM NOW!" I screamed. My speed must have doubled! I was running faster than I had ever run before.

A wise person once said "Don't give up the things and people you love." That wise person, she was my mum. She always told me to follow my dreams. She told me this on her death bed. I'll never forget her. She was the only part of my family that truly cared about me. Red Flame is my family now. I can't lose them. I WON'T lose them!

Suddenly I ran into Aiden. Before he knew it I had grabbed his arm and was pulling him behind me while I was running full speed.

"Resha, what are you doing?!" he yelled.

"If you and Kat don't make up... Red Flame is finished," I yelled. Tears came running down my cheeks. Aiden looked at me shocked and then he laughed.

"Kat and I have already made up," he smirked. I stopped in my tracks and turned around to face him.

"What!" I said.

"We already made up. Feral already told me about Red Flame disappearing and everything."

At first I was shocked and I felt all my energy leave me. I must have used it all running. I passed out.

"Resha!" yelled Aiden.

I woke up in the nurse's office. I didn't have my eyes open but I could hear. "Wait, what happened?" said a voice that sounded like Kat's.

"Feral had told her about Red Flame disappearing if we didn't make up," said another voice which sounded like Aiden's.

"Did she tell you this?"

"No, I used my magic to read her mind. She was panicking so I told her that we made up and then she passed out," said Aiden's voice.

Kat groaned. "You do know that's an invasion of privacy?"

"Forgetting that, I want to put the past behind us and be a team again," said Aiden's voice.

"Agreed!" said Kat's voice.

After hearing that, I couldn't help but open my eyes and smile. "I'm glad you two are friends again," I said. Kat and Aiden suddenly turned to look at me.

"HOW LONG HAVE YOU BEEN AWAKE?!" they yelled.

"All of it," I smirked.

Kat grabbed the pillow and started hitting me with it. "This is for listening in on stuff you shouldn't," she yelled. "And this is for making me and Aiden worry about you!" she said, hitting me with a pillow. Aiden was worried Kat was smothering me with the pillow but all I could do was laugh.

My new family was the best! They cared about me, and they laughed with me. Red Flame may be violent, weird, spooky and strange and lots of other things. But all that matters to me is the fact that they care about me and like me for who I am and not who I'm born as! If I'm right I might be able to tell them who I really am soon... I couldn't have chosen a better school to go to!

Chapter 8:

Memory Magic!

Most people have pasts they want to keep locked away. Pasts that they don't want anyone else to know or see. But I have learnt it's better to share them with your friends or keep them bottled up.

"Hey guys!" shouted Malica, running into the classroom. Since the incident when Kat and Aiden almost led the whole school to destruction Lucas and Malica have joined our team. Lucas still doesn't get on well with Aiden but other than that everything is normal.

"Guys, the Master asked us to tidy up the Magic Library," said Malica.

"Magic Library?" I enquired.

"It's a special library filled with books about magic," replied Lucas.

"For some reason nobody has been allowed in it for five years," said Aiden.

"Gramps must really trust us if he is letting us tidy up," added Kat with gleaming eyes. "I'm fired up!" she yelled as she was surrounded by flames.

"I wonder why no-one's been allowed in?" I asked curiously.

"Does it matter? Let's go!" Kat shouted, pulling all of us behind her.

The magic library was a mess! There were books on the floor everywhere. I had a bad feeling about the place but I didn't want to worry anyone. I picked up a book and climbed up the ladder to put it on the shelf. Everyone started doing the same thing.

All of a sudden, I saw a spider and screamed. I lost my balance and knocked a book off the shelf. Lucas, Aiden, Kat and Malica all tried to catch me but we ended up in a bundle on the floor. The book which I knocked down fell on the floor open.

Suddenly there was a flash of light and we were bundled on the floor in the middle of a street. The book was sitting about a metre away from us wide open. No-one seemed to notice us or the book. Someone came walking towards us but, as if he was a ghost, he walked right through us. We got up. Malica gasped. "What is it Malica?" I asked. She pointed towards a building. It was Red Flame! But it was different.

"It's the school ten years ago," gasped Lucas, Kat and Aiden.

Suddenly two girls and two boys came out of the school. Malica gasped. "It's us!" she yelled. She was right! The two girls had a really close resemblance to Kat and Malica. The boys also looked a lot like Aiden and Lucas. The boys started fighting which proved even more that they were Lucas and Aiden.

The girl with red hair and goggles who looked like Kat smashed their heads together. "Will you two grow up!" the girl said. By the looks of things nothing had changed much. Aiden and Lucas start shouting at Kat who looked a bit embarrassed at what had happened. The littler versions of them were fighting too. Little Malica looked sad. The big Malica was also looking sad, as if she knew why. The little Malica started running in the direction of the town church. Malica ran after her.

"Guys, come on!" I yelled while running after the big Malica.

When we got to the church the little Malica was crying. We all looked at the Malica from our time. Suddenly she fell to her knees and burst into tears. "Mama! Papa! Come back!" cried the big Malica. "This was the day my parents... died," she cried. Everyone started to feel a bit sad.

"Don't cry... they've not gone," said Kat. "They're always with you."

Malica stopped crying. She looked up at us. "I-I... I know," she smiled.

The background changed. What was once a church changed to an icy waste land. We couldn't feel the cold for some reason. In the distance we could see a boy.

When he got closer we realised it was Lucas! He had no top on as usual but how could he stand the freezing cold like that?! He was walking like it was nothing! Suddenly the boy fell to his knees. He whispered something. Lucas looked disturbed. As if this was a memory he would rather forget.

"IT'S ALL MY FAULT," the boy shouted.

Lucas also fell to his knees. "Sis... Lil sis," he whimpered. "I... I couldn't save you," he cried. "This was the day... I... couldn't save..." We all comforted him and then the background changed again.

This time it was a forest. "Sister!" a voice called. Suddenly the boy who looked like Aiden came running. He then tripped over a tree stump. "Sister... where are you?" the boy cried while lying on the floor. Aiden looked like he knew what was going on.

"This was the day Kat and I got split up," he said.

Kat hugged him. "I'm sorry," she responded in a soft voice. I didn't know what was going on but it looked personal so I decided to keep out and so did the others.

Without any warning the background started to change again. This time we were in a carriage. I knew straight away that it was my past. Sitting opposite us was a little girl. That little girl was me. She had the same doll I had. I knew what day it was and what the memory would be. It was the day I decided to try and join Red Flame. Suddenly the horses went berserk. The carriage was being pulled along. The girl fell to the floor of the carriage. I looked out of the front window and waited for it. Unexpectedly a lady with blonde hair came flying past the front window onto the driver's seat. The only thing that I truly remembered from that day was a hand with the Red Flame sign on it. When the carriage had stopped the lady ran off. All I could see as she ran was her blonde hair and the Red Flame sign on her hand. I was on a hill just out of town. From there you could see the Red Flame School. "This is me... and this is when I wanted to join Red Flame," I said.

Chapter 9:

A Past Long Forgotten

"Strange, at this time we would have been in Red Flame, but I don't remember a girl with blonde hair," said Aiden.

"Looks like it's my memory next," said Kat. She didn't look a bit scared, like she had nothing to hide. But I guess that's because she was always with Aiden.

As it had before the background changed. We were in a dark forest. Kat's face expression changed instantly, like she was scared. In front of us was a building.

It had a mark like Red Flame on the front door. "Is it a wizard school?" I asked.

"I've never seen this symbol before," replied Malica.

"Not this memory... anything but this," added Kat, who was trembling. Whatever this memory was about it must have been bad to get Kat scared.

Suddenly a little girl who couldn't have been more than six ran out of the building. She ran past us but tripped. We saw her hair was red and instantly knew it was Kat.

"This... this is the day I used magic for the first time... and the day... I got this scar," said Kat holding her hand over her fringe.

All of a sudden, a man came walking out of the building. He was laughing. "Where do you think you're going, Rat?" he laughed. "You know you can't get away."

The girl looked up. "Let me go," she responded quietly.

The man just laughed. "Now we're going to have to punish you for trying to run away again," he said. He held up his hand and lightning crashed around it.

"No," the girl whispered. "LEAVE ME BE! I JUST WANT TO BE LEFT ALONE FOR ETERNITY!" she shouted. The man used his lightning magic on her and she was sent flying. Her body looked lifeless on the floor.

She then stood up. "I have had it," she said with her head facing the floor. "No-one will ever boss me around AGAIN!" she shouted. Her head shot up revealing her new scar. She opened her mouth and flames shot out. The man couldn't run. The flames engulfed the whole forest in less than a minute flat.

When some of the flames cleared the girl was the only living thing left. She was on her knees facing the ground in amazement. If you looked close to the flames that surrounded her it looked like they were talking to her. Comforting her, "don't worry... we're your friends... with our help... no-one will ever boss you around again..."

"They made me feel at ease... they made me come to realise what happened... and they were always there for me..." she said.

"Who were?" asked Malica.

"The flames," replied Kat.

Her eyes started to fill up with tears. We were shocked. Kat wasn't the type to cry so easily so this must have been a bad experience.

Our attention turned to the girl, who had started to mumble something. Suddenly she looked up. Her eyes were blood red. "Red Flame... they will look for him... my only human friend... Aiden," the girl said. Her eyes turned back to blue. She got up and started running. "I ran... I ran all the way to Red Flame... to look for you Aiden..." Kat said.

The background disappeared and we were in complete darkness. Kat fell to her knees on the floor.

"I feel like such a wimp," she joked sarcastically. Aiden hugged her.

"Don't, it's good to let your feelings out once in a while. After all, it's your weaknesses that make you stronger."

Kat started letting out a stream full of tears and cuddled her twin. I couldn't help but start crying too. I fell to the floor and joined the hug.

"It's all right to cry. We've all had bad times," I added. Malica started to cry too and she joined the big hug on the floor. Lucas was trying to hide the fact he was crying too, but I noticed. I held my arm out. He looked at it with teary eyes. "We're a team now, right?" I enquired. "One person's happiness is everyone's happiness, one person's anger is everyone's anger and one person's tears are everyone's tears." Lucas crouched to the floor and cried but refused to hug. Malica and I then pulled him into the group hug.

Suddenly there was a flash of light and we were all huddled on the floor in a bundle like we had been before. The book started falling again. Kat grabbed the book before it fell on the floor and closed it. She put the book on the shelf.

"I've changed my mind, how about we go on a job instead?" she laughed. Everyone nodded eagerly and ran out of the library.

We all agreed to forget what happened in that room but I could never. After all, thanks to that book our team grew closer and stronger too!

Chapter 10:
Community service

Our next job was in Beachville. Beachville, as you may have guessed from the name, had the most wonderful beaches. The team had agreed to go to the beach after the job, but it was more like a 4-1 majority vote. Kat refused to go to the beach because of the water, sand and swimsuits.

"That's pretty much everything that's fun about the beach!" I said.

"That's why I hate the beach," Kat responded sourly.

"Come on, it'll be fun!" added Lucas.

"You just want to see me in a bikini!" she snapped back.

"WHY WOULD I WANT TO DO THAT!" he shouted.

"Lucas... you're blushing though," said Malica.

"Is it the fact that you're embarrassed about wearing a bikini?" I whispered.

"HELL NO! IT'S THE EXACT OPPOSITE!" she shouted.

"Well whatever the reason is, it's decided," I responded.

"Whatever, let's just get on with the job," replied Kat walking off into the shop.

"Aiden," said Malica, Lucas and I all at the same time. "Kat hates being seen as a girl."

"She says boys underestimate girls," added Aiden walking in after Kat.

"Well she's got us there," responded Lucas. Malica and I followed in after them.

The shop was, coincidentally, a swimsuit shop. It sold trunks for boy and swimsuits and bikinis for girls. As soon as Kat realised this she was horrified. But to make it even more bad for her, all employees had to wear swimsuits that were sold in the shop.

"That's it, I quit," said Kat walking towards the door.

"Wait, I need as many workers as possible!" the owner responded.

"Don't care," replied Kat.

"I'll pay everyone ten times the asking price!" he shouted. Kat stopped in her tracks and turned around.

"TEN TIMES?!" she shouted. "THAT'S LIKE TWO MILLION JEWELS EACH!" she yelled. Then she stopped. "Swimsuit... two million jewels!" she said counting her fingers. "Fine," she sighed.

The girl who worked there gave us swimsuits that would fit us and we went to change. Everyone was changed before Kat, which wasn't a big surprise. I had a blue bikini on and Malica had an orange one. Aiden was wearing green trunks with star, which really suited him, and Lucas was wearing a pair with an ice pattern on. But he always went around topless so I saw no difference.

"Kat hurry up, our shift has started," said Malica.

"I don't want to!" Kat shouted.

"You better come out Kat or we're coming in for ya!" I yelled.

"Okay, okay!" she shouted. She pulled back the curtain and stepped out. Her bikini was a red and black camouflage pattern. Her hair was up like it always was with her goggles in her hair and her fringe was still hanging over her left eye. We all gasped in amazement. No-one would have thought she would look so hot in a bikini, but to be fair I think nobody who's seen her in a bikini has ever lived to tell the tale. "Stop staring, you perverts!" she shouted angrily.

"Wonderful, just wonderful," clapped the manager.

"You look so girly in that." Kat was not thrilled by this comment. You could see in her eye she was getting the urge to punch the manager in the face.

Aiden ran over to her and put his arm over her shoulder. "Well let's not stand here forever, we have work to do!" he said smiling.

Aiden and I were working the tills while the others showed of the swimsuits they were wearing and pointed out outfits the costumers would look good in. I had never seen so much anger and hatred in Kat's eyes. It was like she was about to blow a fuse.

But no-one else could have fitted into the category 'Beach Babe' better than she did. Even with the anger in her eyes, the smile she put on made everyone want to buy some swimsuits. Plus being the Kat she is, she couldn't help but ask Lucas to turn the floor into ice and slid across it on a surf board like she was really surfing. This made costumers want to buy stuff even more. She put up a volley ball net and started to play a game with Malica in the store! But again it just made people want to buy more. The Manager was extremely happy with the result that her carefree attitude had on the customers.

Chapter 11:
Bye-Bye Beachville!

The day was going pretty well. When not many people came into the store Kat was asked to put some more swimsuits on the empty racks while everyone but Malica and I took a break. They only went into the back room for a cup of coffee though. The door then opened and three boys stepped in. I was half asleep on the counter due to the long day and Kat wasn't in the mood to entertain costumers so Malica went up to them.

"Welcome, can I help you?" she asked. One of the boys grabbed her and started touching her up. I had fallen asleep on the counter and they covered her mouth so Kat didn't hear her. But the leader of the boys made the biggest mistake of his life. He went up to Kat.

"Hey there," he said. She ignored him completely.

"Hey you! Are you deaf or something?" he yelled.

Kat looked towards him. "I'm sorry, but can I help you?" she replied.

The leader and one of the other guys were blocking Malica from her sight. "Yeah, I was wondering if you were free tonight?" he asked flexing his muscles.

Kat looked away. "I'm sorry but this is a swimsuit store not a 'pick-up-a-girl' store," she responded.

"You clearly don't know who you're messing with! I'm the leader of the Black Jack gang," he shouted with an angry looking face. Kat finished hanging up the swimsuit that was in her hand and turned to face the guy.

"I am really not interested in who you are, or what gang you're from, but one clear detail I have picked up about you is you're not very sharp."

Her Red Flame mark which was on her right cheek was in full view plus she and her brother were known worldwide as the Red She-Devil and the Blue Eclipse. There was known to be only one redheaded girl in Red Flame and that was her.

The boy got angry. He was about twice the size of Kat with the size of his muscles not included. He brought his hand up and pushed it down as hard as he could to squash her.

"KAT!" screamed Malica, who had got her mouth free. The boys in the back heard this and ran to the shop. There was a cloud of dust everywhere.

When it cleared you could see Kat holding the boys in her hand one inch away from her head with ease. I woke up and saw this sight. Kat looked up at the guy.

"You made a big mistake today, a mistake that's going to haunt you for the rest of your life. My name is Kateline Flamebuster; also known as Kat. I'm The Red She Devil from Red Flame Wizards' School." The guy looked scared. "First, you violate my friend, then you hit on me and then you try to hit me and that will not be tolerated," she said. Her eyes then turned red. The boy tried to back out the door but it was too late.

"FIRE MAGIC: FLAME QUEEN!" she shouted. Her fringe flew to the side revealing her scar and the crown of flames appeared on her head. She shot forward using flames and hit the boy in the face using Fire Fist. She kept battering them until her magic energy ran out. She then passed out from the lack of energy and Lucas caught her.

I looked around the city. "We've gone and done it again... we've destroyed a whole city!" I said. The city was rubble.

"Hey Resha, reminds you of when we first met?" laughed Aiden.

"Sure does," I smiled.

"Well let's repeat that," he added. Everyone started running as fast as possible. Lucas had also started running while carrying the unconscious Kat. And if you listened really carefully, between our panting and running you could hear the army just like on the first day we met, a day no-one will be able to forget!

Chapter 12:
Council Threats

"You destroyed another city!" shouted Layla. Aiden and Lucas started grumbling and Kat started to smirk and looked away from Layla.

"Yeah, we did," Malica replied.

"You guys are nuts," sighed Layla.

"It just proves even more that they should be in a zoo!" smirked Lilith, who was walking past. Kat punched her in the face and sent her flying into the back wall.

"You wanna say that again, Porky?" shouted Kat.

"Settle down class," said Miss Elimenmo as she entered the room. Everyone took their places. "We have bad news. Due to all the trouble you've caused the school is being shut down!" she cried.

"WHAT?" said the whole class.

Kat stood on her table. "No way I'm going to let us be shut down!" she shouted.

"Yeah Miss!" shouted Aiden as he jumped on his table.

"There's nothing that can be done. It's the Magic Council's ruling," she cried. Swiftly the class grew quiet. Kat and Aiden sat back in their seats looking a bit glum.

The Magic Council is very powerful. It's full of powerful wizards. Those powerful wizards make judgement on magic-based issues that a normal government wouldn't be able to do anything about. The issue this time must have been Kat and the rest of us rampaging through cities. I felt kind of responsible for what happened.

"It's my fault," came a voice at the back. Kat was once again standing on her table. "It's my entire fault, I'm the one to blame!" she said. "So why is everyone else getting punished? We all love Red Flame and I'm not letting them take it!" she shouted. She ran to an open window in the classroom and jumped out.

As she was Kat, the girl who destroyed two towns with only the help of her twin brother, there was no doubt in anyone's mind that she wouldn't have landed safely. Everyone ran to the windows to see what she was going to do. She started running.

Suddenly I heard a window open and Aiden jumped out of it. "You two ladies coming to rescue not just our school, but our friend?" Lucas whispered into mine and Malica's ears. We both nodded. Lucas grabbed a hold of us. "Hold on tight now," he said. He jumped out the window and made a slide of ice for us.

When we reached the ground the slide disappeared and Lucas let go of us. "Let's go!" I shouted. Lucas, Malica, Aiden and I all started running. We were all heading to the same destination. The Magic Council!

Chapter 13:

Flickering Flame

We were all still running but there was no sign of Kat. "Damn it, I hope she doesn't do something stupid," said Aiden. I felt like he just jinxed it. We arrived at the council tower that was located outside of the town. There was a massive hole near the entrance.

"Looks like she beat us here," I groaned. I started to walk towards the tower but Aiden put his arm out to stop me. I looked at him confused.

"That hole wasn't made by Kat," he replied. "Kat may not think before she acts but she knows how to make an entrance. She knows the council is located at the top of the tower, so she would have shot up to the top using her fire as a boost..."

"... then she would make a hole up there, correct?" finished Lucas.

"Exactly," added Aiden.

"But then who made the hole? And where is Kat?" I asked. Suddenly there was an explosion at the top of the tower. A body came flying out of the tower and something dropped to the floor.

"It's Kat's goggles!" shouted Malica.

"So that's..." said Lucas looking at the falling body.

Without any warning the body turned over to face the tower and fire shot out of its legs. "Yeah, that's our Kat," I said. She vanished back into the smoke coming out of the tower. A few seconds later she was sent flying only this time she was sent downwards. She didn't have time to boost back up so she landed on her feet and she supported herself with her right hand.

"Kat!" I shouted. She then looked at me as if she hadn't noticed we were there.

"What kept ya?" she smirked.

"What's going on?" asked Lucas. "You aren't fighting the Magic Council, are you?" questioned Malica.

"Far from it," replied Kat standing up. Her trouser and top had been ripped to shreds. If it wasn't the council she had engaged in combat... then who was it?

"The Magic Council is off today," groaned Kat. "Lucky sods though... if they had been

here the Eagle Claw might have got 'em,"
she said.

"Eagle Claw?" I asked.

"A dark wizards' school for dark
wizards... nasty scum," said Lucas.

"You mean you were fighting ..." started
Malica. All of a sudden, there was another
explosion only this time it was near the
bottom of the tower. We were sent flying.

Malica and I both flew into trees. The
others were just pushed back a little. From
the smoke infested hole came three figures.
Malica and I jumped up and joined the
others. "Oh look, more flames for us to play
with," said one of the Eagles.

Kat had her hatred-filled stare pinned on
the tallest one. "Well, well, look what we got
here," said one who looked a lot like a
player wearing glasses.

"State your names!" demanded Aiden.

"I'm known as Crow," said the one who had spoken first. He wasn't very interesting; in fact he could have fit into any crowd with ease.

"I'm known as Blackbird, and if you want an autograph you'll have to beat me," he smiled while pushing his glasses up. He looked like he wanted girls to notice him. He wore sunglasses. I thought I was about to throw up and Kat couldn't resist laughing. "I see, you think I'm so good looking you're laughing at the other boys," said Blackbird.

"Ha ha, you're so full of yourself," Kat responded bursting into laughter. "You have a face not even ya mother could love," and Kat continued to roll about on the floor laughing.

Malica and I couldn't help but laugh too. "Why it is the boys are the only ones who understand hotness?" questioned Blackbird. Suddenly, out of nowhere, even though there was no sign of them cracking or even trying to hide their laughter, they fell on the floor laughing. Blackbird was about to step forward but the tallest stopped him.

"I'm known as Eagle, the strongest in Eagle Claw," he said. Kat stopped laughing and her head shot up. She then stood up.

"That's enough messing around," she said. Everyone got up and slowly stopped laughing.

"When she's serious it's never a good thing," I added.

"So now we've told you who we are, who are you?" said Eagle.

"I'm Malica," replied Malica.

"Lucas," responded Lucas.

"I'm..." I started. I didn't want my identity to be revealed in front of my friends. "I'm Resha," I added proudly. Luckily neither Eagle Claw nor my friends seemed to realise.

"I'm Aiden, also known as Red Flame's Blue Eclipse," said Aiden.

"The legendary Blue Eclipse in person," responded Crow.

"And I'm Kat."

"Hey Eagle, isn't a girl with red hair, blue eyes and the name Kat..." started Crow. Eagle's eyes opened wider.

"The Red She-Devil," he said in amazement.

"Are we that famous already Bro?" asked Kat sarcastically while putting her arm on his shoulder and smirking.

"Guess so," replied Aiden.

"The twins from hell..." added Eagle.

"What a tragic fate for such a beauty, destroying everything she touches," said Blackbird.

"Call me a 'beauty' again and it'll be your face that gets destroyed," smirked Kat while setting her hand alight.

"Violent as well," smiled Blackbird.

"I will take you on, She-Devil," said Eagle.

"I'm fired up!" smirked Kat.

"Resha, Malica, you guys stay back," added Aiden.

"Okay," replied Malica and I. We ran behind a tree to make sure we didn't get caught in one of Kat's explosions.

"I'll take on the pretty boy, you handle Crow," said Lucas.

"Pretty boy? How dare you!" yelled Blackbird.

"Oh, so you're having a temper tantrum?" Lucas laughed.

"Fine, I'll take on Crow," added Aiden.

"Let's get this party started!" said Kat launching forward at Eagle.

Chapter 14:

The Battle of Flames

The battle then began. "Why would you even think about insulting Kat like that?" asked Lucas. "I would never insult a lady," replied Blackbird.

Lucas hit him in the face and he went flying into the tower wall.

"There you go again. Kat's no lady ... she's a violent, carefree, fire eating flame!" said Lucas.

"You fail to see true beauty," responded Blackbird, getting up.

Out of nowhere Kat punched him in the face. "I told ya not to call me a beauty!" she shouted. She ran back off to attack Eagle.

"Ha you had that coming!" added Lucas.

Blackbird slowly got up. "Not once... but twice... my beautiful... face!" he shouted.

All of a sudden his body shape-shifted which meant his body was transforming into someone or something else; he then transformed into a tiger.

"A shape-shifter, huh?" said Lucas. Lucas was attacked by the tiger but he had managed to dodge it. Then he turned the floor to ice and the tiger slipped over. Then the tiger turned into a penguin. "A penguin?" questioned a surprised Lucas. The penguin slid on the ice towards him. At the last minute it turned into a polar bear. Lucas couldn't dodge it and was hit by the polar bear. "Darn it," said Lucas. He slid back on the ice. "He can shape-shift pretty fast." The polar bear broke the icy surface then changed into a lion.

Luckily Lucas looked like he had an idea. He waited for the lion to pounce at him. He jumped into the air. "ICE MAGIC: ICE CAGE!" he shouted. Then he went full-pelt downwards towards the lion. Suddenly a huge cage of ice surrounded the lion. Lucas was sitting on top laughing. "This is how I caught the last shape-shifter too," he smirked.

He jumped down from the top and landed in front of the cage. "ICE MAGIC: ICE BOMB!" he shouted. In his open hands appeared a bomb made of ice. He attached it to the cage and ran over to Malica and I. "ICE MAGIC: MAGIC SHIELD!" he said. A big shield of ice appeared between us and the cage. Suddenly there was a big explosion and it wasn't Kat. Lucas removed the ice shield. The Blackbird guy was lying on the floor unconscious.

"Way to go Lucas!" I shouted.

Aiden's fight had been going differently. Aiden hadn't used his magic once. He was just hitting, kicking and dodging but it was very effective.

"Why don't you use your magic?" asked Crow.

"Because you have no magic to fight back with," smirked Aiden holding up a crow ring that he had been wearing earlier. Crow looked at his hand where the ring had first been and he looked back at Aiden. Without any warning Aiden kicked the guy in the face. The guy was very weak in physical strength and was unconscious in an instant.

"What a weakling," I said. Aiden ran up behind Kat during her battle.

Her fight wasn't going as well as the others. Even though she had become a lot stronger than when I first met her. She was being sent flying like a rag doll.

"This is all the famous Red She-Devil has to offer?" questioned Eagle. Kat was slowly getting up from the last attack. She wasn't looking too good.

"Lucas I need your help," said Aiden.

"Got it," replied Lucas running over.

"We need to do a Magic Tenrisa," Aiden added.

"Let's do it!" responded Lucas. A Magic Tenrisa is when two or more wizards combine their powers to make a third sort of power that one wizard alone can't possess. Little did I know they were going to make not just a third sort of power but a fourth that can be held by one wizard for a short amount of time!

"Star Magic; Magic Tenrisa," said Aiden.

"Ice Magic; Magic Tenrisa," added Lucas.

"Magic Tenrisa; Ice Star," Aiden and Lucas shouted at the same time. Suddenly a star covered in ice appeared. Stars are naturally made of fire. So for it to be surrounded by ice is truly the work of a Magic Tenrisa.

The star of ice was located just in front of Kat. "What is the point of putting it near her?" laughed Eagle. Kat took a piece of the star and ate it. The star wasn't very big but it was big enough for Kat to eat in two bites.

"What are you doing?!" asked Eagle.

Kat finished eating the star. "Now I'm fired up!" smirked Kat. What looked like blue lightening surrounded her.

"This is the effect a Magic Tenrisa between star and ice magic can have if eaten by a fire wizard," added Aiden.

"Fire Magic; Queen of Flames," Kat said. Her fringe flew to the side revealing her scar. Her eyes turned red and the crown of flames appeared. Blue lightening still surrounded her. She had never looked more terrifying, she flew forward and Eagle tried to block her but he got burnt. Kat had beaten him to a pulp.

Chapter 15:

A Fairy Tale Ending!

Kat's magic energy ran out and she passed out. Lucas ran over and caught her before she hit the ground.

"We made a big mess," said Malica.

"I'll fix it," I responded. I stepped forward and picked one of the roses in my belt. "ROSE MAGIC: MEND!" I said. I threw the rose at the tower and all of the bricks on the floor slid back in place as if it had never been destroyed.

"Good work Resha," nodded Aiden.

"No biggy," I replied.

"Looks like we had better be getting back," said Malica.

"We will have to try saving our school another day," added Aiden. We all started to walk back to school. The next day we had got news from the Council.

"Our school isn't going to close!" said Miss Elimenmo who was in tears of joy.

Apparently one of the Council members had been watching our fight with Eagle Claw and had shared the information with the rest. The Council had decided that Red Flame wouldn't close down. Everyone was overjoyed.

After school, the rest of the team and I went to the hill where you could see Red Flame and the whole city. The sun was setting. It looked wonderful. I sat down on the hill. "I can't believe six months ago I had only just met you guys," I said. Aiden sat down next to me.

"Yeah who would have thought?" he laughed.

"It seems like we have known you forever," smiled Kat.

"I can't wait for our next adventure as a team," said Lucas.

"May be we will destroy another town," laughed Malica.

We all started laughing. I could tell just within that moment, that we would have so many adventures together... and I just couldn't wait!

After that things went pretty smooth. My magic got a lot stronger and so did Malica's! Kat is still ripping up towns here and there.

Lucas and Aiden have become better friends but still have small fights to see who is stronger. Things always seem to be turning upside down. But I guess that's Red Flame Wizards' School for ya!